Jimbo, *originally a stowaway, but Captain Roger allowed him to join the crew as ship's boy*

Flashfork, *ship's cook. He is no master chef but the crew rarely complain; he's a hot-tempered man, armed with a cutlass and a rolling pin!*

Anne, *the daughter of Bessie, landlady at the inn on Pirate Island. She is a fearless pirate and loves to take part in Darkshark's adventures whenever she can*

Spinoza, *the mischievous ship's monkey and* **Popsy**, *Captain Roger's faithful and very talkative parrot*

On the large island of Sabatina, somewhere in the Tropical Sea, lives Governor Broadside with his sister Aunt Prudence and niece Camilla.

Life is never quiet for the Governor and his men as they try to keep law and order in the territory. The seas are full of pirates, pirate ships and pirate adventures, with Captain Roger, Bo'sun Will and the crew of the Darkshark constantly pitting their wits against their arch enemies, Captain Foul and the crew of the Barracuda.

British Library Cataloguing in Publication Data

Grant, John, *1930-*
    Captain Roger's birthday.
    I. Title   II. Silcock, Sara
    823′.914[J]
    ISBN 0-7214-1310-2

First edition

Published by Ladybird Books Ltd Loughborough Leicestershire UK
Ladybird Books Inc Auburn Maine 04210 USA

® LEGO is a registered trademark belonging to the LEGO Group and is used here
    by special permission.
© LEGO GROUP MCMXC
© LADYBIRD BOOKS LTD MCMXC
Printed in England

Captain Roger's Birthday

by JOHN GRANT
illustrated by SARA SILCOCK

Ladybird Books

Captain Roger paced *Darkshark*'s quarterdeck. He could see the man at the wheel and the look-out in the crow's nest. The rest of the crew were nowhere in sight.

"Idle scoundrels!" he shouted. "Stop skulking and get on with some work!"

The pirates heard the Captain shouting. They were crowded round Bo'sun Will in the hold, having a secret meeting.

"Remember," Will was saying, "it's a secret. The Captain mustn't find out that we're giving him a surprise birthday party."

"With mountains to eat!" said Flashfork.

"Gallons to drink!" said Rummy. "Hornpipes! Shanties! Arm wrestling! Broken furniture!"

"And sore heads in the morning!" cried the rest of the pirates. "Wonderful!"

A few days later, *Darkshark* sailed into Pirates' Nest. Will and Rummy slipped ashore and hurried to the 'Keg and Cutlass'.

"Bessie!" shouted Rummy. "Bring food and drink! The best you've got! We're going to surprise the Captain with a birthday party!"

"There's some cheese," said Bessie, the landlady. "I've a few ship's biscuits. Maybe half a pot of coffee."

"Ship's biscuits? Cheese?" cried Will. "This is a party! We need more than that!"

"There was more," said Bessie. "But it's all gone.

"When
Captain Foul
and the crew
of the *Barracuda*
captured that treasure
ship the other day, they
had a party to celebrate,
and cleaned me right
out of supplies."

"Perhaps we can buy some food at the store," said Will. They hurried to Magpie's General Store.

"Sorry," said Magpie. "I can let you have a carrot and two potatoes. Foul and his crew went off with everything else."

The pirates were very downhearted. They had been looking forward to a party. Then Will had an idea.

"Who is the greediest person we know?" he asked.

"Governor Broadside!" cried the pirates.

"That's right," said Will. "All we have to do is to trick the Captain into sailing for Fort Sabre, then we can creep ashore and steal some booty for the party!"

Back on board, Will knocked on the Captain's cabin door. "We're in luck, Captain," he said. "There's news ashore of a treasure ship headed for Fort Sabre!"

"Well, don't just stand there!" shouted Captain Roger. "All hands to make sail! Cast off!"

"He's fallen for it," Will whispered to Rummy.

Three nights later, *Darkshark* lay at anchor off Sabatina Island. There had been no sign of any treasure ship. And Captain Roger was in a very bad mood.

Under the cover of the dark, Will, Rummy and Jimbo rowed ashore. Popsy sat on Jimbo's shoulder. They crept up to the walls of Fort Sabre. High above was a lighted window. They could smell cooking.

"We can't possibly get up there," said Rummy.

"Popsy can," said Jimbo.

Popsy flew up and landed on the windowsill. Inside, Governor Broadside was at supper.

"Today's report, please, de Martinet," he said, stuffing another forkful of turkey into his mouth.

"The reinforcements have arrived," said the Lieutenant. "Dragoons with, of course, their horses." Supplies had arrived, too, with the soldiers. Lieutenant de Martinet read from a long list. But the Governor wasn't listening. He was staring at the open window. Suddenly he gave an angry yell.

"Parrots! I detest them!" he shrieked. And he slammed the window shut.

Poor Popsy squawked and flew down to Jimbo. She preened her ruffled feathers, muttering, *"...enough to feed a hundred...twenty barrels...in the wagons...on the quay..."*

"Crazy bird," whispered Rummy. "Keep her quiet! The guards will hear!"

"She's trying to tell us something," said Jimbo. They listened.

"She's been eavesdropping," said Will. "Someone up there was talking about food. Enough to feed a hundred… twenty barrels? That could mean beer. Or wine. Or…"

"Or rum!" said Rummy.

"I bet it's supplies for the Governor's birthday party," said Will. "He and the Captain were born on the same day, you know. Remember, last year the Governor had a banquet and fireworks! Come on, we must tell the others to prepare for a raid!"

They rowed back to the ship.

"The treasure ship has been and gone," reported Will. "But the cargo is on the quay at Port Royal."

Darkshark set sail and dropped anchor in a quiet cove. Then Will, Rummy and a dozen others went ashore, armed to the teeth!

The Governor's wagons waited on the quayside. The drivers sat laughing and chatting with one another. A group of soldiers stood guard.

Will whispered to the pirates, "Rummy and I will grab the guards. The rest of you deal with the drivers."

The pirates gave a loud yell, and leapt out waving cutlasses and pistols. The fight did not last long. The soldiers saw that they were outnumbered and quickly surrendered, and the drivers were too scared to move. The pirates tied them up, and did the same with the soldiers.

"Quick!" shouted Will. "Get the wagons unloaded!"

The pirates climbed onto the first wagon, which was loaded with large boxes. They were marked SHIRTS and BOOTS and BOOT POLISH.

"Where's the food?" cried Rummy.

There was another box, marked GOVERNOR BROADSIDE – STRICTLY PRIVATE.

The pirates took it to one of *Darkshark*'s boats waiting by the quay.

Will ran to the next wagon and lifted the cover. He stared in astonishment. He ran to the next, and right along the line of wagons.

"Rummy!" he shouted, "the wagons are loaded with…"

But, before he could utter another word, there was a loud shout.

It was Captain Foul and his crew.

"Looking for treasure?" he roared. "You can't fool me. I saw you sneaking away from Pirates' Nest!" And with that, he led the crew of *Barracuda* in a wild charge towards the wagons.

To Rummy's amazement, Will jumped up on a wagon and shouted, "Retreat!"

Rummy waved his cutlass. "But... but...!" he spluttered.

"Retreat! Back to the boats!" cried Will. And he grinned and winked at Rummy.

"He's up to something," Rummy realised. And he joined Will in shouting to the puzzled pirates, "Retreat! Retreat! Back to the boats!"

Foul and his crew were taken completely by surprise. They watched as the *Darkshark* pirates ran across the quay and scrambled into the ship's boats.

"Just as I always thought!" jeered Foul. "Cowards, every last one of them!"

A cable's length from the quay, Will told the men to stop rowing. In the moonlight they saw Culverin, *Barracuda*'s first mate, drag the cover off a wagon and climb up.

"What is it?" shouted Captain Foul. "Gold? Diamonds? Pieces of eight?"

"It's hay!" cried Culverin. Other wagons were uncovered. "More hay! Tons of it!"

"Just as Popsy said," laughed Will. "Enough to feed a hundred! A hundred hungry horses!"

A *Barracuda* crewman had run to the last wagon. "Captain!" he cried, "this isn't hay. It's barrels. One, two, three... twenty barrels!"

"Barrels of doubloons, I'll wager!" laughed Captain Foul. "A pity Roger's men weren't brave enough to defend their treasure!"

The barrels were heavy, but the pirates managed to get one balanced on the side of the wagon.

"Careful!" shouted Captain Foul.

He was too late. The barrel fell to the ground...and burst! But it wasn't gold doubloons that showered in all directions. It was tar! Black, sticky tar for the Port Royal dockyard.

Will and his men roared with laughter as they rowed back to the *Darkshark*.

Captain Roger was angry when he heard that the treasure had turned out to be hay. But he laughed when Will told him about Captain Foul and the tar.

"You see, Captain," said Will, "we wanted to give you a surprise birthday treat. But it's a bit past your birthday now."

"There's still the surprise present," said Jimbo fetching a long paper parcel. The Captain opened it.

It was a wooden leg, beautifully carved and decorated with mermaids and pieces of eight.

"Thank you all very much," said Captain Roger. "I'll wear it only on very special occasions."

"And there's a box," remembered Will, "with the Governor's name on it. Maybe it's his birthday present."

It was a giant birthday cake, with pink and white icing and candles, and flavoured with rum.

So, Captain Roger had a birthday treat after all. There was no broken furniture, and only a few sore heads. But still, he declared, it was as nice a birthday treat as a pirate Captain could wish for.

THE TREASURE ISLANDS

JOHN SILVER ISLAND

THE TROPICAL SEA

Darkshark, Captain Roger's ship

FORT SABRE

PORT ROYAL

SABATINA

FENZANCE

PIRATE'S HAT ISLAND

SHARK ISLAND

ISLAND OF FOGS